Autumn
Publishing

Published in 2019
by Autumn Publishing
Cottage Farm
Sywell
NN6 0BJ
www.igloobooks.com

Autumn is an imprint of Bonnier Books UK

0919 003
2 4 6 8 10 9 7 5 3
ISBN 978-1-78905-543-6

Printed and manufactured in China

STORYBOOK COLLECTION

Autumn
Publishing

Contents

A FROZEN ADVENTURE

The kingdom of Arendelle was a happy place, located next to a deep fjord.

At night, the Northern Lights often lit up the skies in beautiful patterns.

But the king and queen lived with a secret worry.

Their eldest daughter, Elsa, had magical powers. She could freeze things and create snow, even in the summer!

Their youngest daughter, Anna, just adored her older sister. The two loved to play together in the snowy playgrounds that Elsa created.

One night, Elsa's magic accidentally hit Anna. The king and queen rushed the girls to the realm of the trolls for some magical help. The trolls advised that Anna would recover. They also advised that Elsa's powers would get stronger, so she should learn to control them.

Back in Arendelle, Elsa struggled to stay in control of her powers at all times. She decided to stay away from Anna, to keep her little sister safe.

The trolls had changed Anna's memories, so she didn't remember Elsa's magic. Instead she grew up thinking that Elsa wanted nothing to do with her.

By the time Elsa was crowned queen, the sisters had grown far apart. They hardly knew each other at all.

Having grown up mostly by herself, Anna had felt lonely for a long time. So
she was thrilled to meet handsome Prince Hans on the day of Elsa's coronation.

Anna and Hans liked each other straight away. At the coronation party they danced and talked all night long.

Anna thought it was a great idea to get engaged quickly. But Elsa reacted angrily. "You can't marry someone you've just met!"

Anna argued back. "I can't live like this anymore!
I'm always alone!"

Then Elsa got upset and an icy blast shot from
her hand – in front of everyone!

Worried that her secret was exposed
and afraid she would hurt someone, Elsa
fled from the castle. Everything froze
behind her as she ran away.

Once Elsa had climbed up into the mountains, she felt calm. Now that she

was all alone, she was able to let out her powers for the first time ever!

She created whirls of snow, ice and even an ice palace.

She was able to be herself and it felt wonderful!

Meanwhile, Anna realised that Elsa had been acting distant for all those years because she needed to hide her magic. Anna decided to go after Elsa – now that her secret was out, they could be together!

Anna headed up the mountain, but her horse threw her into the snow. Luckily, she was able to find shelter in a nearby shop.

Inside, Anna met a young man covered in frost. He was cross because he was an ice harvester and the mid-summer snowstorm was ruining his business.

He also knew where the storm was coming from. That meant he could take her to Elsa!

The young man was called Kristoff, and Anna hired him to take her up the North Mountain to find Elsa.

His reindeer, Sven, came along on the journey, too.

As they neared the top of the mountain, the trio saw a beautiful wintery landscape. Elsa had covered everything with glistening, sparkling ice.

Elsa had also created a
snowman... who was alive!

The snowman's name was Olaf and he was excited to
hear that Anna planned to bring back summer because
he loved the idea of warm weather.
He offered to take them to Elsa.

As the group moved on
they found the fantastic ice
palace that Elsa had created
with her magical powers.

Anna was impressed by Elsa's powers and sparkling ice palace. But she really wanted Elsa to come back home.

Elsa thought the people of Arendelle wouldn't accept her – and she was still afraid that she would hurt them.

The two girls argued.

Although Elsa didn't intend to hurt Anna, she hit her sister in the chest with a blast of ice.

Then she created another snowman, named Marshmallow, who was much bigger than Olaf. The huge snowman made sure that Anna, Kristoff, Sven and Olaf left the mountain quickly!

Once they were safe, Kristoff noticed that Anna's hair was turning white.
Kristoff took her to the trolls to see if their magic could help.

The trolls explained that Elsa's blast had hit Anna in the heart – and that soon
she would freeze completely! But, they added, "An act of true love will thaw a
frozen heart."

Olaf and Kristoff decided to hurry Anna back to Arendelle so she could get a
true love's kiss from Hans.

Meanwhile, in Arendelle, Hans helped everyone during the storm. Then Anna's horse returned to Arendelle – without her!

Hans took a group out to find Anna... but they found Elsa first. Elsa was forced to defend herself against some of the men.

Finally, she was taken back to Arendelle as a prisoner! The men were convinced she was dangerous.

Kristoff brought Anna to Arendelle, but Hans refused to kiss her. He didn't love her! He only wanted to rule Arendelle but had to make sure the sisters were out of the way first.

Anna was devastated. But Olaf realised that Kristoff loved Anna – so his kiss could still save her.

Anna made her way towards Kristoff.

Then she saw her sister in danger…

Anna threw herself in front of Elsa, just in time to block a blow from Hans's sword.

At that moment, Anna transformed into solid ice. The sword shattered against her icy body.

Stunned, Elsa threw her arms round Anna and cried. She didn't want to lose her sister.

Suddenly, Anna began to melt. Anna's act of true love for her sister meant that the spell was broken!

Then, with Anna's love and faith, Elsa managed to bring back summer.

The sisters hugged and promised to love each other from then on. The people of Arendelle saw everything and they welcomed Elsa home.

Kristoff decided to stay in Arendelle and so did Olaf – with the help of a little winter cloud to keep him cool.

Best of all, the sisters were back together and happy at last!

Kristoff excitedly led his friends into Troll Valley.

"Every year at the crystal ceremony, Grand Pabbie honours the young trolls who have earned all their level-one crystals," he explained. "It's a huge achievement."

With each step, Queen Elsa's and Princess Anna's curiosity grew.

They couldn't wait to experience this mysterious tradition for themselves.

"They're here!" Bulda said, when she saw the group of friends. The valley popped to life as trolls rolled out to greet them.

"Kristoff!" a young troll named Little Rock shouted, running to hug him. Little Rock was set to be in this year's ceremony. "I can't believe it's finally time!" he said.

"Can you tell us more about the ceremony?" Anna asked.

"It has to be performed during autumn under the Northern Lights. And we only have a few more days before the last night of autumn," Bulda said before repeating an old troll saying. "Guardians of Earth know autumn lights and crystals glow so our bond may deepen and grow."

Anna whispered to Elsa, "Did you understand that?"

Elsa shrugged. "Troll wisdom can be very confusing."

Anna noticed Little Rock
holding several items in his hands.
"I like your crystals," she said.

Little Rock proudly explained
the meanings of each of his glowing
crystals.

"What about that one?" she asked,
looking at one that wasn't lit at all.

"My tracking crystal," he explained.
"It won't glow until I have excellent
tracking skills. If I can't earn it, I can't
be in the ceremony."

"But I don't understand," he continued. "I've been tracking all kinds of things, like caterpillars and bugs."

"Little Rock," said Kristoff. "You need to venture out of the valley and use what you've learned. Tracking is more than just following."

But the idea of leaving the valley alone made Little Rock nervous.

"To be a good tracker you need to be fearless, be observant and even be inventive sometimes," said Kristoff. "I know you can do it."

"I'll try," said Little Rock. "But I'm not sure—" Suddenly he gasped. "Look at those clouds! If we can't see the Northern Lights, there won't be a ceremony!"

Then he looked around for Grand Pabbie… but the old troll was nowhere in sight. None of the other level-one trolls were there, either! "Where is everyone?" Little Rock asked nervously. "Did they forget me?"

"Don't worry," said Bulda. "I'm sure Grand Pabbie just went to find a new site where the lights are visible."

"Why don't we track him?" suggested Kristoff. "Maybe you can earn your crystal."

Little Rock's frown spread into a smile.

"A REAL tracking quest? With all of you? Yes!"

"That could be a long trip," said Bulda. "You better take some warm cloaks so you don't get cold!" Quickly, the trolls dressed Anna, Kristoff and Olaf in cloaks of moss and leaves. Elsa politely declined because she never felt cold.

"I feel like a forest," said Olaf happily, spinning in a circle.

He didn't notice his cloak fly off, landing high up in a tree. But being made of snow, he didn't need it anyway.

As they headed off, Elsa pointed out wisps of Northern Lights in the distance. "Maybe we should head that way?"

"That's what I was thinking!" said Little Rock, as he hurried to take the lead.

When the path split three ways, Little Rock paused.

He looked back at Kristoff helplessly.

Kristoff pointed to the first path.

"That goes back to Troll Valley," he hinted.

Little Rock stepped towards the second path.

"That's towards Arendelle," said Anna.

He confidently started down the third path. "This way!"

Suddenly, Little Rock stopped. "I'm picking up a scent."

"Trolls have an incredible sense of smell," Kristoff whispered to the others.

"I think it's Grand Pabbie!" Little Rock dropped to the ground and began sniffing along a trail… straight to a hoof.

"Um, that's Sven," Kristoff said gently.

Little Rock tried to cover his mistake with a joke. "Sven! Stop standing on Grand Pabbie's footprints!"

Elsa could see that Little Rock was nervous, so she thought a story might be just the thing to ease his mind. "The Northern Lights make me think of the amazing beauty of nature," she said as they continued up the mountain.

"What do the lights make you think of, Anna?"

Anna smiled at her sister.

She knew exactly what Elsa meant.

"One night, long ago," began Anna. "Our parents took us to the top of a huge mountain, hoping we'd get a great view of the Northern Lights."

"We had never been up so high," said Elsa.

"Or up so late!" added Anna.

"We were playing hide-and-seek under the light of a full moon until, suddenly, these pink and green ribbons of light rippled across the sky," said Anna.

"The Northern Lights!" exclaimed Olaf.

"Yes!" said Anna. "Then we ran up a steep hill to get higher!"

Elsa smiled. "Actually, I used my powers to make a staircase out of snow! It was like we were running up into the sky."

"When we reached the very top, a snow flurry fell around us," said Anna.

"Sitting there together with the lights and the stars and the glittering snow…"

"It was amazing," Anna and Elsa said together.

"See, Little Rock?" said Elsa. "New experiences maybe scary at first, but if you're fearless, they can turn into fun adventures!"

As the group reached a frozen river, Kristoff reminded everyone to walk carefully. "I don't know how solid the ice is."

"Don't worry," said Little Rock. "I did complete my ice trekking crystal. And this is definitely thick enough—" *CRACK!*

The ice split beneath Little Rock's feet! Anna and Kristoff grabbed him.

"Elsa! Remember the story? Maybe a stairway can get us across,"

Anna shouted.

Elsa quickly got to work. The group watched as a swirl of ice began to form into a stairway arching over the river.

They ran up the steps, but when they started to descend they heard a rumble. The riverbank beneath Elsa's stairway began to break off.

"I don't know what to do!" Little Rock cried. "I think this is a level-two crystal challenge!"

Thinking fast, Elsa waved her arms. Sheets of ice appeared and when their fronts curled up and froze – they looked just like sledges! "Jump on!" Elsa shouted.

Everyone swooshed down the steep arch! Picking up speed, they raced down the frozen river.

As the sledges slowed to a stop, the friends whooped happily. They had made it across the river.

Little Rock smiled up at Elsa and Anna.

"You saved us! I want to be fearless just like you," he said.

He gave them a glowing crystal from his pouch.

"You deserve to carry this."

Elsa and Anna admired the beautiful crystal.

Determined to be a fearless leader like his friends, Little Rock declared, "This way to Grand Pabbie!"

"That's back to the river," whispered Kristoff.

Little Rock spun around. "I meant, this way!" he said, marching in the opposite direction. The others smiled. They were sure Little Rock would find Grand Pabbie and the Northern Lights, and get his tracking crystal to glow – even if he did need a little help!

Elsa felt excited and worried in equal measure. Tomorrow was her sister Anna's birthday – and it was the first one in many years that the sisters would spend together!

Elsa rose early, while Anna was still sleeping, and began the preparations for the big day. She decorated the castle courtyard and used her magical powers to create a beautiful icy topper for the cake.

Kristoff, Olaf and Sven soon arrived to help. They had made a birthday banner, which they hung across the courtyard.

Elsa tried not to panic as she watched the wet paint drip from the banner on to the tables below!

"Are you sure I can leave you in charge here?" Elsa asked Kristoff.

"Absolutely," he replied.

Elsa headed off to finish the decorations, but then she caught sight of Olaf sneaking a taste of the birthday cake!

"Olaf, what are you doing?" she asked.

"I'm not eating cake," said Olaf.

Elsa leaned close to him. "It's for Anna," she said with a smile.

Just then, the morning bells chimed and Elsa hurried inside the castle to wake the birthday girl.

"Keep an eye on that cake!" she called to Kristoff, and dashed into the castle.

Elsa sneaked quietly into Anna's room. "Pssst. Anna," she said.

Anna yawned. "Yeah?" she said, her eyes still closed.

"It's your birthday," said Elsa.

At first, Anna was too sleepy to realise what Elsa was saying, but then…

… she sat straight up!

"It's my birthday!"

While Anna changed into her new birthday dress, Elsa suddenly sneezed and two tiny snowmen appeared. They were snowgies! The creatures fell to the floor and scampered away before the sisters even noticed them.

With a magical wave, Elsa added flowers to her own dress and ice sparkles to Anna's. Although Elsa's head felt a bit funny, nothing was going to stop her from making Anna's birthday really special.

Next, it was time for Anna to find her presents!

"Just follow the string," said Elsa, handing the end of it to her sister.

Anna sprinted down the hall, eager to see where the string would lead her.

Anna followed the string down the hallway…

…and under some furniture.

She quickened her pace…

… until she ended up at a suit of armour, where she found a beautiful bracelet!

Next, the string led to a cuckoo clock. But instead of a cuckoo, it had a tiny Olaf figure which shouted "SUMMER!" every time the clock opened its doors.

Next there was a huge, delicious sandwich and then a brand-new family portrait.

The sisters were having lots of fun, even though Elsa's sneezes were becoming more and more frequent.

Anna was worried, but Elsa insisted that she was feeling fine.

Neither of them noticed the tiny snowgies that continued to appear with each sneeze…

Back in the courtyard, Kristoff and Sven were busy with the decorations when suddenly a group of the little snowgies appeared! They stared at the tiny snowmen in disbelief.

The snowgies jumped all over the place and made the punch bowl topple over! Elsa was not going to like this!

Olaf, on the other hand, was very excited to meet these tiny new friends!

"Ah-choo!" Elsa sneezed again as she and Anna zipped down the stairs on Anna's new bicycle.

By now, Anna was worried that Elsa had a cold.

"I'm fine," Elsa said.

Elsa had even more gifts for Anna outside the castle. They stopped at Oaken's kiosk, where its owner was busy having a sauna!

Oaken gave Anna his softest cloak, then offered Elsa a cold remedy that he said was 'of his own invention'.

"No thanks," Elsa said, taking a deep breath of the steamy air.

"We'll take it," said Anna.

Anna's final present was at the top of the tall clock tower.

"Now we climb," said Elsa.

"You need to rest," said Anna. But Elsa insisted.

Elsa grew more tired with every step. At the top, way up high, Elsa suddenly twirled feverishly – and almost fell!

Anna caught her poor sick sister. "You've got a fever. You're burning up," she said, determined to get her sister to rest.

Meanwhile, more and more snowgies were arriving in the courtyard and causing chaos! One group knocked down the birthday banner and Olaf had to re-hang it.

"All fixed," Olaf announced, putting up the last piece.

DRY BANANA HIPPY HAT

A second group of snowgies headed for the birthday cake.

Kristoff tried to stop them...

… but the snowgies seemed determined to destroy the cake. This time they launched themselves at it!

Kristoff had promised Elsa he would keep the courtyard in order, and he didn't want to let her down.

As the sisters reached the doors to the courtyard, Elsa turned to Anna.

"I'm sorry, Anna," she said sadly. "I just wanted to give you one perfect birthday."

"Everything has been absolutely perfect!" Anna said, pushing open the doors…

"Surprise!" called Kristoff. He had managed to sort everything out just in time! Even he was amazed.

Anna's eyes lit up at the sight of the decorations, her friends and the hundreds of tiny snowgies. "Wow!" she said.

Everyone sang 'Happy Birthday', then Kristoff slid down off Sven's antlers and knelt before Anna with her birthday cake.

Anna had a huge smile on her face.

Using his antlers, Sven cut the beautiful cake into slices for everybody to enjoy.

Elsa was proud of all the hard work she had put into the day.

But she felt another sneeze coming on. Elsa really needed to get to bed…

73

… but not before doing one last thing.

In Arendelle, there was a huge birthday horn, which the king or queen would blow on special birthdays. Anna tried to stop her, but Elsa was determined!

As Elsa blew into the horn, she accidentally sneezed and sent a giant snowball flying far across the ocean…

… and right into Hans! It knocked him off his feet!

At long last, Elsa let Anna
take her up to her bedroom.
It was finally time to rest.

In Elsa's bedroom, Anna gave her big sister some warm soup.

"Best birthday present ever," said Anna.

"Which one?" asked Elsa.

"You letting me take care of you," said Anna.

The sisters smiled widely at each other. It really was Anna's best birthday ever, and it was all thanks to Elsa and their wonderful friends.

High on the North Mountain, not long after the birthday party had ended, Marshmallow opened the doors of the ice palace for Kristoff and Sven. Olaf came running in, surrounded by the little snowgies! Everyone had decided the ice palace was the best place for them to live.

Kristoff looked at Marshmallow, shook his head, and said, "Don't ask."

TROLL TREK

Princess Anna was reading a story to the village children.

"'That night, the young trolls climbed the highest mountain and grabbed the stars out of the sky. They tossed the stars to each other and bounced them off the moon.'"

Turning the page of the book, Anna continued.

"'The dancing lights woke the humans. They gazed at the stars shooting across the heavens, admiring the display and wondering what was causing it. Suddenly, the lights stopped and everything was still again.'"

Anna sat down to finish the story.

"'Back in the Land of Trolls, the troll parents had discovered what mischief their children had made and demanded they put the stars back.'" Anna turned to the last page of the story. "'And the little trolls obeyed… sort of.'"

Delighted, the children clapped their hands.

Troll Trek

"Are trolls really real?" a girl named Mari asked.

The rest of the children began to chatter.

"No way," shouted one child.

"My grammy saw one in the barn once," said another.

Anna smiled. "They're not quite like
the trolls in the story, but they're real,"
she said. "Just ask Kristoff."

Kristoff cleared his throat. "I've never known any trolls that could grab stars, but yes, they are real."

"How do you know?" asked a boy.

Kristoff told them he was raised in Troll Valley. All of the children gasped.

"Where's Troll Valley?" Mari asked.

"I can't tell you," said Kristoff.

"It's a secret."

The children groaned in disappointment as they collected their things and prepared to leave. But Mari lingered behind.

She approached Kristoff. "Do you mind if I ask you a few questions?" she said.

Kristoff agreed, and Mari took out a notebook. She eagerly asked him things like, "Did you grow up by a stream?" and "What types of flowers did you smell during spring?" and "Is it true that trolls sleep all day?"

Mari wrote down everything he said.

"We have many books on trolls," Anna said. "You can borrow some if you'd like."

Mari followed Anna towards a large bookshelf in the corner of the royal library.

"All of the troll books are right here, on the lowest shelf of this bookcase," Anna said.

Mari flipped through the books. Troll stories had always been her favourite and she wanted to know everything about them. But most of all, she wanted to find out for herself if trolls were real.

After hours inside the royal library, Mari headed home with an armful of books.

She stayed up late, reading and trying to separate fact from fiction. When she found an ancient map that mentioned trolls, she studied it and used her notes from her talk with Kristoff to create a map of her own.

The next day, Mari woke up bright and early. She finished her chores as fast as she could, and without saying a word, she grabbed her things and left.

It wasn't long before Mari's parents realised she was gone. They were devastated, thinking she was lost. They rushed to the castle. When they heard that Anna and Elsa hadn't seen Mari that morning, Mari's mother broke down in tears. The sisters immediately gathered others to help search for Mari.

As the villagers set out to look around the kingdom for the lost girl, Anna, Kristoff and Elsa packed for a longer trip. They were certain that Mari had gone out in search of the trolls. "I had no idea this was what Mari had in mind when she asked me all those questions," Kristoff said.

The three friends hurried into the mountains. "Do you think she'll make it to Troll Valley?" asked Anna.

"I'm not sure," Kristoff said. He suggested they talk to Grand Pabbie, the leader of the trolls. "He'll know what to do."

On the way to Troll Valley, they looked for Mari but saw no sign of her. When they arrived, Kristoff approached a large boulder that unrolled, revealing Grand Pabbie. "Have you seen a little girl wandering around?" Kristoff asked.

"I have not," said Grand Pabbie. "But I will help you find her."

"Can I come?" a young troll named Little Rock asked. "My tracking skills have improved. I can find her."

Grand Pabbie nodded. "You may join me."

"Yes!" exclaimed Little Rock, hopping with excitement.

"You cover the east side of Troll Valley and we'll cover the west," Grand Pabbie said to Kristoff, Anna and Elsa. "Then we'll meet back here."

And with that, the group split off in search of Mari.

Meanwhile, Mari was walking up the mountain. She stopped beside a twisted, knotty oak tree. When she heard the gentle sound of water, she traced her finger across her map. Kristoff had mentioned a stream. "Aha!" she said.

Mari followed the water for quite a while before seeing the same knotty tree. "Oh, no," she said. "I just walked in a circle."

She looked up at
the setting sun and
began to wonder if
searching for trolls had
been a good idea.

Mari took a deep breath and sat down to examine the map more closely.

As Little Rock and Grand Pabbie reached the top of the hill, they spotted her and stayed out of sight.

"Wait… balancing rock formation…" she mumbled. "That's what I missed."

Little Rock and Grand Pabbie had an idea as Mari started off again. They would secretly help her find the way.

Mari gasped when she saw a rock formation just up the hill. She wondered how she'd missed it before. "Maybe I'm closer than I thought!" she said.

Grand Pabbie and Little Rock continued to create the landmarks on Mari's map without her ever seeing the two of them. In no time at all, Mari was on track to reach Troll Valley.

When the other trolls saw the group coming, they rolled themselves up into boulders, creating the edge of a pathway for Mari.

When Mari stopped to feel a patch of soft green moss on what
she thought was a boulder, she tickled a young troll's head.
The troll had to try his best not to burst out laughing!

Mari got the strangest feeling that something, or someone, was guiding her. *Maybe it's troll magic,* she thought.

She decided to test her theory and suddenly turned and walked towards the slope of the hill.

Mari had to look twice when she saw a pile of big rocks appear below the edge of the hill as if to prevent her from falling. *Definitely troll magic,* she thought. *I must be close!*

Just then, Anna, Kristoff and Elsa approached. "Mari!" Elsa called to her.

Anna gave Mari a hug. "I'm so glad we found you."

"You shouldn't be out here alone," said Elsa. "Everyone has been very worried."

Mari hung her head. "I know," she said. "I'm sorry. I won't do it again. I just wanted to find the trolls."

Mari looked over at Kristoff. "So… is this where you were raised?"

Suddenly, Kristoff's adoptive mother, Bulda, popped open and

blurted out, "Of course it is! He lost his first tooth right here!"

"You *are* real!" Mari gasped.

She gave Bulda a hug. When the trolls came out of hiding, Mari knew they had helped her find Troll Valley. "All of you were with me!"

They nodded and smiled. Mari greeted each one, and vowed to remember all of their names.

That night, after Anna, Elsa and Kristoff had led Mari back to her grateful parents, Mari decided to create a troll story of her own. Visions of all the wonderful things she could include in her very own troll tale filled her head as she drifted off to sleep.

THE GHOST OF ARENDELLE

One afternoon, Anna and Olaf were in the royal library when Olaf spotted a large pink book.

"Ooh! I like this one!" Olaf said. "Wait. What's it about?"

Anna read the title aloud: "How to Find a Ghost."

"I love ghosts!" Olaf announced. "What's a ghost?"

"Well, it's…" Anna smiled and put her book down.

"I have an idea. Follow me!"

Minutes later, Anna and Olaf burst into Elsa's office.

"Elsa!" Anna said. "Olaf wants to learn about ghosts, and I think—"

"We should have an indoor campout and go looking for one!" Elsa finished.

"Exactly!" Anna said.

Hours later, Elsa gathered some snacks from the kitchen.

She packed some fruit and pink marshmallows.

Anna grabbed lots of pillows and blankets from their bedrooms to make their indoor campout as comfortable as possible. Then, they met Olaf and began to look for a dark, spooky room they could use.

They ended up in an old, unused portion of the castle.

"I can't wait to learn about ghosts!" Olaf said.

"Let's make a fire to roast the marshmallows first," Anna said.

"Ooh, I just love warm fireplaces!" Olaf declared.

After the sisters had eaten their fill of roasted marshmallows, and Olaf had created a sticky marshmallow tower, they settled down with their blankets and pillows.

"Is it time to learn about ghosts?" Olaf asked.

"Yes," Anna said. "You go first, Elsa!"

Elsa laid the book on her lap and began to read.

"'Long ago, on a dark night in Arendelle…'" Elsa whispered. She continued with her story as Olaf listened, wide-eyed.

A while later, Elsa heard a snort. It was Anna. She'd fallen asleep.

"Well, Olaf, I guess my ghost story made Anna pretty tired. Come to think of it, I'm tired, too!" Elsa said as she yawned and snuggled down under her blanket. "Maybe we'll find a ghost tomorrow."

"I'd like to meet a ghost," Olaf said before blowing out the candles.

Soon both sisters were sound asleep.

But Olaf couldn't rest. He wanted to meet a ghost as soon as possible!

As he looked at the pictures in the book, he remembered something Elsa had read to him. Apparently, ghosts got lonely and wandered around at night.

"Sometimes I get lonely and wander around at night, too!" Olaf said.

"Maybe the ghost and I could wander together!"

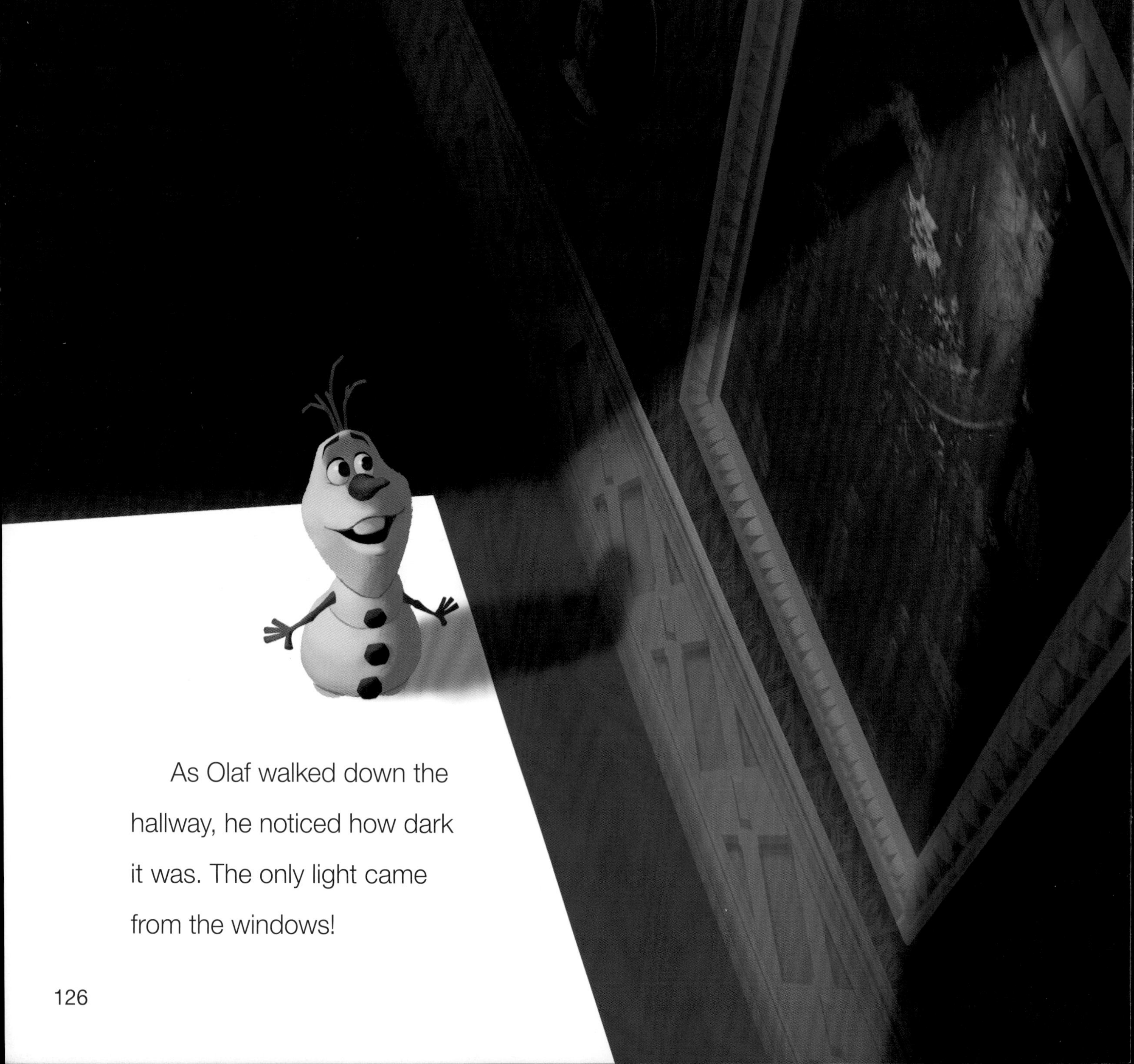

As Olaf walked down the
hallway, he noticed how dark
it was. The only light came
from the windows!

He looked right and he looked left. He looked up and down.

But he didn't see any ghosts.

"Hello?" Olaf said aloud. "Ghost? I'm here to be your friend!"

Nobody answered.

Olaf turned a dark corner at the end of the hallway, and then...

... Thump-thump-thump.

Thump!

Olaf tumbled

down a
staircase!

THUMP!

Anna and Elsa woke with a start.

"What was that?" Anna and Elsa asked in unison. Then, "I don't know!" they exclaimed quietly.

"And where is Olaf?" Anna asked.

They got up and put on their shoes. Elsa lit some candles

and they wandered out into the hallway.

"Oooh!" came a little voice from the
bottom of the staircase.

Anna gasped. "That sounded like—"

"A ghost?" said Elsa.

They crept down, down,
down the stairs.

"Hello? Are you there, Sir Ghost?" Elsa said.

"We want to be your friends!" Anna added.

"Oh-oh-oh! I want to be friends, too!"

the ghost said.

Anna and Elsa stopped short.

"Are you ghosts?" the ghost said.

"Wait…" said Anna suspiciously.

"Do you like warm hugs?"
asked the ghost.

"Yes," said Elsa, "we do like warm hugs. Are you—"

"Olaf?" Anna asked.

Elsa quickly pulled off the sheet.

"Oh! I can see again!" Olaf exclaimed. "Thank you, ghost that looks just like Elsa!"

"I am Elsa!" she replied with a laugh.

"Oh, okay," said Olaf. Then he pointed to Anna.

"And you are…?"

"Anna," said Anna.

"Olaf, you made this our best ghost hunt ever!" said Anna.

"But I didn't find any ghosts," Olaf replied.

"Well, maybe you didn't, but you became the best ghost-like snowman we've ever seen!" Elsa declared.

THE END